Mommy, Who Made Me?

Emily Faircloth

PAGE PUBLISHING
Conneaut Lake, PA

First originally published by Page Publishing 2024

ISBN 979-8-88654-729-0 (pbk)
ISBN 979-8-88654-743-6 (digital)

For Brandon, whose love, support, and
encouragement pushed me to publish my work.

For Cooper and Rowan Kate, whose curiosity and
imagination allowed for all kinds of teachable moments.

Cooper was wide-eyed and full of wonder, as many young frogs are.

He had one burning question, though, and knew the answer wasn't far.

So Cooper asked his mother one day, "Mommy, who made me?"
Mother replied gently, "Look about, and you will see."

Cooper saw Mr. Rabbit next and asked, "Can you tell me please?"
"I need to know who made me." Rabbit answered, "the Maker
of the seas."

Cooper next hopped into Mr. Tortoise and asked his question on the way.

Tortoise smiled and answered slowly, "He Who made night and day."

Cooper decided he'd keep asking until certain he wasn't wrong. He asked Mrs. Robin the same question. She added, "He Who gave me song."

As Cooper looked into the pond,
Duck asked, "What's on your mind?"
He sighed very softly, "I want to
know the Creator of my kind."

Duck suggested visiting Wise Old Owl in order to be quite sure.

So he was off to find Old Owl, remembering what all the other answers were.

He found Mr. Skunk on the meadow road.
Cooper's heart still carried the heavy load.

He asked, "Who made me?" with all of his might.
Skunk beamed, "He Who painted me black and white."
Skunk continued, "And I may add this as well:
It is He Who fashioned my powerful smell."

To Wise Old Owl's tree Cooper finally came,
After Owl's answer, he'd never be the same:
"Well, my dear, I'm glad you asked. Set your eyes high above.
The King of kings and Lord of lords has made you out of love.
He knows every note you've not yet sung.
And knows the length of your long, sticky tongue."

And the answer Cooper sought from the very start
Had been there all along deep down in his heart.

Now if you listen carefully at night, with others, you'll hear Cooper sing
Sweet serenades of celebration, for he's a child of the King.

"You will seek me and find me when you seek me with all of your heart. I will be found by you," declares the Lord.
Jeremiah 29:13-14a

About the Author

Emily Faircloth is a professional educator and a certified school counselor. From raising her own children to working with students of a variety of ages and across multiple settings, she wholeheartedly believes in the power of teachable moments embraced by the healthy and purposeful curiosity and wonder of a child. These moments help foster growth and creativity and provide an opportunity for children to discover and utilize their beautifully—and wonderfully—unique, God-given gifts and abilities. Emily resides in Sulphur Springs, Texas, with her husband, Brandon. They have two children, Cooper and Rowan Kate.

9 798886 547290